Kin's Deepest Desire…

Kin watched from the pit wall with Scuffs, fascinated, as Waddy accelerated into the first turn.

The blue and yellow Taurus seemed to stretch out like a greyhound as it ducked low into the corner and ran flat out down the long straightaway.

The unmuffled roar of the powerful Ford V-8 was like a song of power and speed.

Watching the sleek stock car, Kin felt a rush through his veins. He could almost imagine the thrill of powering it through the turns.

Someday I'll be out there driving! he vowed silently.

Collect all the
NASCAR Pole Position Adventures:

#1 ROLLING THUNDER
#2 IN THE GROOVE
#3 RACE READY ·
#4 SPEED DEMON ·
#5 HAMMER DOWN ·

·coming soon

ROLLING THUNDER

POLE POSITION ADVENTURES NO. 1

T. B. Calhoun

HarperEntertainment
An Imprint of HarperCollinsPublishers

▄ HarperEntertainment

An Imprint of HarperCollins*Publishers*
10 East 53rd Street, New York, N.Y. 10022-5299

This is a work of fiction. The characters, incidents, and dialogues
are products of the author's imagination, or if real, are used ficti-
tiously. Any resemblance to actual events or persons, living or
dead, is entirely coincidental.

First Printing: October 1998

Cover illustration by John Youssi © *1998*
Designed by Jeannette Jacobs

Printed in the United States of America.

ISBN 0-06-105930-7

98 99 00 01 02 10 9 8 7 6 5 4 3 2

CONTENTS

- - - - - - - - - - - - - - - - -

HAMBURGER PLEASE!

"Go!" Kin Travis yelled out loud.

No one heard him because of the noise.

"Go!" he yelled again.

The noise was all around him, rising and falling like the wild pounding of a storm. Waves of sound blasted his ears, washing over him so that his whole body shook. When he closed his eyes, Kin could almost imagine he was standing on the beach, listening to the breakers crash, watching the lightning dance on the horizon.

RrrrrroooOOOOOM!

When Kin opened his eyes, he saw he was standing by the infield fence of a race track.

The bright shapes whipping past were not lightning bolts, but race cars.

They streaked by so fast that Kin could barely see the helmeted drivers inside, tucked down and strapped into their seats.

VVRrrrrroooOOOOOM!

VVRrrrrroooOOOOOM!

VVRrrrrroooOOOOOM!

As Kin watched, three brightly colored stock cars disappeared around the high-banked first turn. The noise of rolling thunder died to a distant roar. But it would be back. And soon! The cars were halfway around the track behind him.

Like most teenagers, Kin loved noise. He loved the look and feel of speed.

Someday, Kin thought, *I will drive one of those cars. Someday I will be the one flashing past, and not the one watching.*

"Go!" Kin yelled again. It was fun to be watching from the infield. He could yell as loud as he wanted. He could shout until his lungs were sore, and no one would tell him to stop.

No teachers, no social workers, no mournful preachers or sad-eyed relatives.

No Aunt Adrian.

Though Kin loved his Aunt Adrian, he didn't miss her. He didn't miss her cold, elegant house in the Boston suburbs, where everyone spoke in whispers.

Not at all. He liked being here in sunny Tennessee, surrounded by the smells of exhaust and gasoline and cut grass, watching the cars roar past, three at a time.

This wasn't a race day; it was a practice day. Kin had used the pit pass his granddad had given him to get into the infield on his own. The infield was the grassy area in the center of the oval track.

Usually the infield was filled with racing fans. But since today was a practice day, Kin had the infield almost to himself.

Kin liked being on his own. Though it was a little lonely, being the only fifteen-year-old around. He almost missed his little sister and brother.

Almost but not quite.

*   *   *   *   *

VRrrrrooOOOOOM!

A car zoomed past, and Kin followed it with his eyes. It was blue and yellow, and on the side it said PEYTONA RACING.

"Sounds a little lean, don't it?" a voice asked.

Kin jumped; he had thought he was alone.

He looked over his shoulder and saw a boy about his age, hanging on to the fence beside him.

"Lean?" asked Kin.

"That new intake manifold," said the strange teenager. "On the SVO engine. You a Ford man? You can hear the difference, can't you?"

"Oh . . . intake manifold . . . sure thing," said Kin.

He had no idea what an intake manifold was. But maybe if he acted as if he knew what he was talking about, he could make some friends.

The stranger was chewing a toothpick. Instead of jeans and a T-shirt like Kin, he was wearing a brightly colored uniform covered with patches and emblems of various companies and auto parts manufacturers.

They were blue and yellow, the same colors as the car that had just passed.

Kin stuck out his hand. "My name's Kin."

"Junior," said the stranger. "Junior Peytona."

"Are you a driver?" Kin asked as they shook hands. He envied Junior's colorful uniform.

"Almost," said Junior. "That is, I will be someday. I already know how to drive. My dad's Waddy Peytona. That's his Taurus that just passed. I'm on the pit crew."

Junior turned around so that Kin could read the back of his uniform: WADDY PEYTONA RACING TEAM.

"I see," said Kin, trying to sound cool.

As if he met a racing team member every day!

VRrrrrrOOOOOM!

VRrrrrrrrrOOOOOM!

Two more cars roared by, and the boys turned to watch. After the cars had passed, Junior said, "You sure have a funny accent. What kinda name is Kin?"

"It's short for McKinley," said Kin. "McKinley Travis. I'm named after my great-grandfather. He was a pioneer in the Imperial Valley."

"That's in California," Junior said, narrowing his eyes. "Guess that means you're from out West."

Junior spoke in a thick Southern accent. "West" sounded like "way-est."

"Born and raised on the West Coast," said Kin. "But I live in Boston now. Or as they call it, Baah-ston."

"I guess every region has its own accent," said Junior. "I've never been west of the Mississippi, but I've read all about the West. I've read about the high plains, and the dry lakes, and the Rockies and the Sierras. I used to collect geography books when I was a kid. This summer, if we can get a new sponsor, we're going out to California to race. I want to see some real mountains, not just these little puppies."

He pointed scornfully toward the craggy top of Rockcastle Mountain overlooking the track. The mountain looked pretty big to Kin, though he didn't say so.

"And big oceans," continued Junior. "I've seen the Atlantic a hundred times. I want to see the Pacific. It sounds awesome."

"This is my first time down South," said Kin.

"Like it?"

Kin shrugged. "It's not too bad."

"So where are your folks?" asked Junior. "Are they in the racing game, too?"

"Not exactly," Kin said, looking away so Junior wouldn't see the tears that filled his eyes and threatened to spill over. When would he get over that?!

"My dad was a computer hardware designer. My mom was a music teacher. They—died last year. They were killed, actually."

"Oh," said Junior. He looked at Kin with a new respect in his eyes. "A wreck?"

"World Wide Airlines. Flight 888," said Kin.

That was the easy part. Kin didn't need to explain anything. Everybody knew about the tragic accident of WW 888. It was like saying the *Titanic*.

"That's bad," said Junior. "That's real bad."

Kin shrugged. "That's the way it is. That's why I'm here, really. I spend half the time with my aunt in Boston, and now I'm hoping to spend the other half with my grandfather."

"I got an idea," said Junior, grabbing Kin's sleeve. "Let's go get something to eat."

"I thought the refreshment stands weren't set up until race day," said Kin as the two teens walked across the infield.

"Mostly they're not," Junior replied. "Not for the fans anyway. But you're one of us now."

"I am?"

"Of course. That plastic badge around your neck," said Junior. "Do you think they let just anybody walk around in here in the infield? It means you're family."

Family, thought Kin. *I guess the word means different things to different people.* To him it meant something bright and warm in his past—something that was suddenly gone, swept away. Now gone forever.

Still, it was good to have a friend!

Kin followed Junior to a sleek mobile kitchen in the center of the infield. It was covered by a bright awning that read INFIELD ANNIE'S HOME-STYLE EATS.

A stocky, grandmotherly woman with friendly blue

eyes and short black hair stood behind the counter. She was wearing a baseball cap that said THE KING and a T-shirt that also said THE KING.

"I guess she's an Elvis fan," Kin whispered.

"Elvis? Man, are you way off!" Junior whispered back. "This is stock car racing country. There's only one King in stock car racing country, and that's Richard Petty."

"Is he a driver?"

"He was. He retired a few years back, but you still see him around. Now his son Kyle is a driver. And a good one, too. But not as good as I'm gonna be some-day."

The woman behind the counter looked up from her stove. "Hello, Junior," she said. "Who's your pal?"

"His name is Kin," Junior said. "Kin, meet Infield Annie."

Kin stuck out his hand. As she shook it, Annie studied the newcomer.

"You look familiar," she said. "But if you've never been around here, I guess it's my imagination. You boys want something to eat?"

"Yes, ma'am," said Junior.

"A hamburger, please," said Kin.

Infield Annie put two paper plates onto the counter.

While Kin watched, she filled both plates with greens and red beans, and topped them with corn bread.

"I—uh—wanted a hamburger," Kin said.

"Ssssh!" Junior said. "You don't order at Infield Annie's. You just take what she gives you."

WHY PRETEND?

Infield Annie's stand had picnic tables, but Kin and Junior took their plates to the fence, where they could watch the cars streak past while they ate.

VVRRRoooooOOOOOM!

VVRRRoooooOOOOOM!

VVRRRoooooOOOOOM!

Only twenty cars at a time were allowed on the track during practice. The sound was almost like the thunder of a real race: a distant roar, changing into a loud hammering, and then fading out as the cars rounded the high back of turn number two.

VVRRRROOOOOOOOOOM!

Another car flashed by, already slowing. It was midafternoon and practice was over. Some cars were going in while others were heading out.

- - - - - - - - - - - - - - - -

"How come your dad is practicing?" Kin asked. "Is he a new driver?"

"He's been driving for twenty years," said Junior. "Practicing doesn't mean learning to drive. It means trying out different combinations."

"Combinations?" It sounded to Kin like a meal at a fast-food drive-in.

"Tires, shocks, carburetor jets," said Junior. "Plus, every driver wants to try out the track and find the groove."

"The groove?"

"The spot where you can go the fastest. High or low on the turns." He turned and looked at Kin sharply. "Say, don't you know *anything* about racing?"

This guy is being a friend to me, thought Kin. *Why should I pretend?*

"Not really," Kin confessed. "I'm here in Tennessee to stay with my grandfather. I've never been to a race track before."

Junior shrugged. "There's a first time for everything," he said. "I could tell you didn't know much about the track and were sort of pretending. It's dumb, but I do it sometimes, too. My daddy says nobody likes to admit they don't know something. But unless you do, you can't learn anything new."

"Your dad sounds like my dad," said Kin. Then he remembered. "Like my dad was, anyway."

"They all talk alike," said Junior.

RRRoooooOOOOOM!

"Speaking of my dad, there he goes!"

Both boys turned to watch the yellow and blue Ford Taurus roar by.

"Anything you don't know from now on," Junior said, "just ask me. I'll tell you what I know, and we'll learn the rest together."

"Sounds like a good deal to me," said Kin. Maybe he wasn't such a loner as he had thought. It felt good to have a friend. Standing beside Junior in the warm Tennessee sun, he felt almost happy. He felt the best he had felt in eleven months, since the tragic accident that had taken his parents.

* * * * *

—— —— —— —— —— —— —— —— —— —— —— —— ——

"Hey!"

Kin looked down.

Something had just grabbed his corn bread off his plate.

Something small and yellow.

A dog.

"Give that back!" said Kin.

He reached out and pulled the corn bread from the dog's mouth. But the dog wanted it more than he did, and it tore in half.

"Worf!" said the little dog.

"Worf yourself," said Kin as he threw the dog the rest of the corn bread. "You can have it!"

Junior laughed. "Go get 'em!" he yelled.

"Whose side are you on?" Kin complained. "Whose dog is it, anyway?"

"Beats me," said Junior. "They don't usually allow dogs in the infield. He must have sneaked in."

Kin looked around for the dog's owner, but the infield was almost empty, except for himself and Junior.

Kin looked at the dog with new interest. *He's an orphan just like me,* he thought.

* * * * *

"Hear that?!" Junior pulled back from the fence.

"Hear what?" Kin asked. All he could hear was the roaring of the cars as they raced on and off the track.

"That's our Ford," said Junior. "Come on. Let's go to the garage area. Dad will be rolling in for adjustments pretty soon."

He started across the infield toward a fenced-off area filled with racing cars and trailers. Kin followed, glad to have found a friend.

"Worf!"

He looked back. He wasn't the only one who was glad to have found a friend.

The little dog was following right behind.

ABOVE THE CLOUDS

The roar was somehow comforting.

Laura Travis looked out the tiny plastic window. The jet engines were winding up, and the huge airliner was beginning to slowly move away from the terminal.

Laura's little brother sat next to her, with his portable computer on his lap. Airline regulations said he couldn't use the computer while the plane was taking off.

"I'm bored," he whined.

"Read a magazine," said Laura.

Larry, who was called "Laptop" because he loved computers so much, rolled his eyes at his big sister. "Magazines are stupid," he said.

Laptop thought everything that wasn't on a computer screen was stupid. Sometimes Laura thought it was because he was a genius.

At other times she worried about her little brother. Since their parents' death a year ago, Laptop, the youngest of the three Travis children, had retreated further and further into the digital world of video games.

Plus, it was harder keeping up with him without Kin around. Aunt Adrian did her best, but children just weren't her thing. Adrian and her third husband, Smedley, ran an art museum in Boston, and they had little time for children.

"Prepare for takeoff," said the pilot over the loud-speaker.

Laura had never flown before. This was her first time. She had read all the statistics about how flying was so much safer than driving.

But Laura knew better. Her parents had been lost in the tragic crash of World Wide 888. All the statistics in the world wouldn't bring them back.

Laura had assured her Aunt Adrian that she could make the trip with no problem. And that was true. She was twelve, after all. She wasn't afraid of flying. One air tragedy in a family was plenty.

What she hadn't told her aunt was that she hated the whole idea of going South for the summer. Everything she had seen about the South on TV made it look stupid and backward. The people talked funny and dressed like hillbillies.

Soon the engines were roaring and Laura was pressed back into the seat. Instead of being afraid, she felt comforted. It felt almost like a hug—a ghost hug from her mom and dad.

Laura looked out the window and watched rainy, gloomy Boston fall away. The cars and buildings far below looked like toys. It was strange and familiar at the same time. Even though Laura had never flown before, she had seen it on TV and in the movies a hundred times.

There were no surprises. She hoped!

Laura glanced over at Laptop. Her little brother looked perfectly calm, except that his eyes were closed.

She reached out and took his hand. He opened his eyes and smiled at her. Then he remembered that he was almost eight and was supposed to hate his big sister. He pulled his hand away.

Laura let him with a smile. If brothers and sisters never talked and only communicated with a look or a touch, how much easier life would be! It was when brothers and sisters started talking that they started to argue.

Outside the window, clouds were whipping by. Then the plane emerged in a white zone, above the clouds and rain. The clouds that had been dark on the bottom were white on top. The sky was a perfect china blue.

It was like heaven!

For the first time in months, Laura felt close to her parents. It was like they were right beside her. *How strange*, she thought, *that on a plane I should feel the safest of all.*

She nestled back in her seat, letting the sadness that she carried with her wrap around her like a blanket.

Two hours later she woke up.

Laptop's head was nestled on her shoulder.

The clouds were gone, and the ground was getting closer. The plane was flying over a highway and the cars were so close that Laura could see the drivers looking up.

The plane was landing. Laura felt the *bump* of the landing gear, then the rush of the engines as they slowed the plane so it could approach the terminal.

Laptop sat up. "Where are we?"

"Atlanta. We change planes here," Laura answered. She felt blue. In her dream, far above the clouds, she had been with her parents.

Now she was back in the real world again, an orphan, on her way to Tennessee to spend the summer with a grandfather she hardly knew.

The Atlanta airport was fun. An underground railway, like a subway, took the passengers from one terminal to another.

The train was totally automatic. Laura looked, but there was no driver. A robot voice told the passengers to get on and off.

She wondered how long it would be before city buses—or even airliners!—had no drivers.

Laura was enjoying the ride so much that she didn't pay attention. When the robot train stopped at the baggage carousel, Laura realized that she and Laptop had gone the wrong way.

"We have to hurry," she said. She grabbed her little brother's hand and pulled him back onto the train.

"I'm big enough to take care of myself," he said, pulling his hand away. "I don't need a baby-sitter."

"Maybe you are, and maybe you don't, but I'm still responsible," Laura said. "I promised Aunt Adrian I would take good care of you."

"I don't need some girl taking care of me!" Laptop protested.

But he followed his big sister anyway.

At the terminal, they ran up the long escalator toward the gate for Appalachian, the airline that flew from Atlanta to the tiny Tennessee airport where they were going to meet their grandfather.

"I have to go to the bathroom!" Larry said.

"No time," Laura said. "We're running late."

"Flight 32 for Greeneville is now boarding," said a voice on the loudspeaker.

"See?" Laura said. Pulling her little brother behind her, she ran past the last men's room, down the hall to the jetway that led to the plane.

They were the last ones on board.

The flight attendant took their tickets and said, "You two barely made it!"

"I still have to go to the bathroom!" Laptop said as they found their seats on the jet.

"You can go to the bathroom now," said Laura.

"Keep your eye on this," said Laptop, handing her his computer.

As he ran toward the front of the plane, Laura took her seat. She was relieved that they had made their flight. If they had missed it, where would they have gone? Two kids in a strange city! Who would they have called?

Traveling without parents was something Laura knew she would have to get used to. But it didn't mean she had to like it.

Outside, it was raining again. She couldn't wait to

get back up above the clouds, into that white, bright realm that was just like heaven.

She leaned back, remembering that peaceful feeling she had felt above the clouds. She fell asleep, and soon she was dreaming of happier days, when the family had all been together. Mom and Dad, herself and Laptop and Kin . . .

Laura woke up.

The plane was high in the air.

Laura looked out the window and saw a few fleecy clouds. Far below were mountains that looked like crumpled wrapping paper.

"Laptop, look!" she said. She wanted to show her little brother the mountains.

But where was he?

The seat beside her was empty, except for his computer.

Was he still in the bathroom?

The bathroom was in the front of the plane. The door opened—and a fat man came out, straightening his necktie.

Laura stood up and checked the seats behind and in front of her. Laptop was nowhere to be seen!

"Help!" she cried. "Stewardess, help! My little brother is lost!—and it's all my fault!"

WHAT MAKES A CAR GO FAST

By the time Junior, Kin, and the little yellow dog with no name reached the garage area, Waddy Peytona's blue and yellow Ford Taurus was rolling in on the access road.

A uniformed security guard was watching the gate.

"Will he let me in?" Kin asked.

"Sure," said Junior. He pointed to the plastic ID hanging around Kin's neck. "You've got an all-purpose VIP pass. Plus, you're with me. You're family."

There's that word again, thought Kin. *Family*. Was it possible that he would find something at the race track to replace the family he had lost?

He doubted it.

The guard at the gate inspected their plastic

badges, then pointed at the little yellow dog. "No dogs allowed."

"Please, let him in," said Kin. "He's an orphan."

"Looks like a plain old dog to me," said the guard.

"Don't be a stiff," said Junior.

But it was useless. The dog had to stay outside.

"See you later," said Kin as he followed Junior into the garage.

"Worf," said the little dog. He sat down forlornly next to the guard, who ignored him.

The "garage" was a section of the infield surrounded by a chain-link fence. Massive car-haulers—the trailers that carried the race cars and their tools and supplies—were parked in a long line on the asphalt. Every square inch of the garage area was filled with cars, parts, tires, and men at work.

Engines throbbed, sheet metal screamed, hammers and air wrenches clattered and banged. Drivers and mechanics—rivals on the track, but friends between races—joked and kidded with one another.

Kin was all smiles. He sniffed the air. "I like the smell!"

Junior slapped him on the shoulders. "You'll make a racing fan yet. What you smell is gas and oil, and hard work and . . ."

"Junior!" a voice called out. "Get your butt over here!"

"That's my dad's crew chief!" Junior said, grabbing Kin's arm. "Come on!"

As Kin got used to the seeming confusion, he saw that the garage was divided into work areas, each one holding a trailer and a race car.

Waddy Peytona's Taurus had just pulled in off the track. The engine stopped and the driver handed his helmet out the window. Kin was surprised to see that instead of opening the door, he climbed out the window.

"No doors on race cars," Junior explained as he helped the driver out of the car. "Dad, this is my new friend, Kin."

Waddy Peytona was a short, stocky man with narrow eyes like Junior's and a quick, bright smile. He stuck out a hand and Kin grabbed it.

"Hello, Mr. Peytona," he said.

"Glad to meet you," the race driver said in a Southern drawl even thicker than Junior's. "And just call me Waddy, please."

"And this is our crew chief, Cope," said Junior.

He introduced a tall, skinny redhead whose uniform hung loose around the seat and knees.

"Copacetic," Cope said. "Now, Junior, help us get this darn car ready."

"Yessir!"

Kin wanted to offer to help, but the men swarming over the car were moving too fast.

Everyone seemed to know exactly what to do.

The Ford Taurus was covered with glistening decals, most of them advertising the same product: Bluegrass Auto Parts.

While Kin watched, Junior peeled off the letters, wadded them up, and threw them into the trash can.

"We just lost our sponsor," he said. "If we don't pick up another one, we're in trouble."

"Don't worry about it, son," said Waddy. "I'm talking to a guitar company this afternoon. They're interested in sponsoring us, if we can make a good qualifying run. Now, how about you changing those tires!"

"Yessir!"

Junior picked up an air wrench. It looked like a pistol with a hose. He squatted down to take off the left side tires.

Badadadadrrrrrrrr! went the air wrench as it whirled off the lugs.

Kin watched, envious and fascinated. *I wish I knew how to do all that stuff!* he thought.

Cope and another mechanic were consulting over the hot engine, which *ticked* loudly as it cooled.

Several other mechanics were under the car. Waddy joined them, hanging up his fireproof racing suit.

"We need to take a round off the left," he said. "She went from way too loose to way too tight."

"He means the steering?" Kin whispered to Junior.

"He means the suspension—the shocks and springs," said Junior. "But you feel it in the steering. When the car is too loose, it *oversteers*, which means

▬ ▬ ▬ ▬ ▬ ▬ ▬ ▬ ▬ ▬ ▬ ▬ ▬ ▬ ▬ ▬

the rear end will slide out on a turn. When it's too tight, it *understeers*. On a circle track, that means you're fighting the wheel all the time. The car wants to go straight, and the track wants to turn."

"And when it's just right, it's copacetic," said Cope.

"I see why they call him Cope," said Kin.

Waddy's head engine mechanic was a short, slight African-American with gray hair named Tach. "I'm going to set the timing up a little for time trials," he called out to the owner and driver.

"Copacetic," said Cope.

"Have at it, Tach," said Waddy. "You're the engine man."

"New to this?" Tach asked Kin, who was watching intently.

"I sure am," Kin admitted.

"Well, keep your eyes open and your ears clean and you might learn a thing or two," Tach said. "For example: Want to know what makes a race car fast?"

"The engine?" Kin said.

"Right! Six or seven hundred horsepower out of

350 cubic inches. Coax all those horses out of that little barn, and you've got a stampede on your hands!"

"Don't listen to him!" said a voice from under the rear of the race car.

"Huh?" Kin leaned down and saw a little man with a wrench, adjusting a shock absorber.

"Meet Carl, our suspension expert," said Junior.

"All the engine in the world won't do you a bit of good if you can't keep the car aimed in the right direction," said Carl. "It's the suspension that makes a race car fast. Shocks, springs, all fine-tuned for temperature and track. That's what it takes to keep the rubber on the road, which you have to have, or it doesn't make any sense to put the pedal to the metal."

"I see," said Kin.

"Bull!" said a voice from behind a stack of Goodyear racing tires. The speaker was an older man with snow-white hair and sideburns.

"Name's Whitewall," he said. "And I'm here to tell you that what makes a race car fast is the tires. What's the point in putting the rubber on the road if the rubber isn't right? You have to have just the right tire and the right temperature and the pressure for the track. Otherwise, the rest of the team is just wasting its time."

"Close, but no cigar," said a short, fat man who was chomping on a dead cigar. "What makes a race car go fast is the gearing. You've got to get the gearing right in the tranny *and* in the rear end, or it's no go. It has to be perfect for the track, or otherwise you're just out for a Sunday drive, no matter how much noise you make."

Kin's head was spinning. He couldn't believe there was so much science, and so many parts, to a race car.

Just then Waddy rolled out from under the car on his blue and yellow creeper.

"You're all wrong, all of you!" he said. He went to the cooler under the window, took out several soft drinks, and threw one to each of the men in the garage.

"What makes a car go fast is the driver," he said, winking at Kin as he threw him a soda.

"Nonsense," said a familiar voice from the doorway. "What makes a car go fast is the camshaft! When the valves don't go up and down, the cars don't go round and round."

Kin looked up and saw a familiar tall, stooped, gray-bearded man wearing a bright red jacket and hat.

"We've got company, boys!" yelled Waddy as he tossed a can of soda to the man in the doorway. "It's the Merlin MixMaster man!"

"Hi, Grandpa," said Kin.

All the men in the garage turned and looked at Kin. "You didn't tell us Hotshoe Hunter was his grandfather," Waddy said to Junior.

"I didn't know," said Junior. "But now I do."

"This is a quick visit," said Hotshoe. "In fact, it's hardly a visit at all. I came to pick up my grandson."

"Aaaaaw, Grandpa!" said Kin. "I was just learning about what makes a race car fast."

"You're learning from the right crowd," Hotshoe said. "Waddy's got one of the best teams on the circuit, even if he doesn't have the most expensive car. These good old boys can make that Taurus fly, that's for sure. But you and me, we've got to see how fast we can make my old Chevy fly down the highway. We have to meet a plane."

"A plane?"

- - - - - - - - - - - - - - - - -

"At Greeneville Airport," said Hotshoe. "Your little brother and sister are flying in from Atlanta at four."

"Oh no!" Kin groaned. But in spite of himself, he felt a glow of anticipation. Could it be that he actually *missed* his little brother and sister?

Kin followed his grandfather out to the parking lot.

"Who's your friend?" asked Hotshoe.

"Friend?" Kin turned and saw the little yellow dog following him. "Oh, just a little dog I met this morning. Can he come with us?"

"What's his name?" asked Hotshoe.

"He doesn't have a name yet," said Kin.

"A dog has to have a name," said Hotshoe.

"Worf," agreed the little yellow dog.

THICKER THAN WATER

If you had been standing alongside a Tennessee country road on a summer day not long ago, you would have seen a beautiful sight.

You would have seen a cherry-red 1955 Chevrolet Belair hardtop cruising through the green, rolling hills.

At the wheel was a gray-bearded man.

In the passenger's seat was a teenage boy with short brown hair and bright eyes.

And in the back seat, looking out the window, was a little yellow dog. If dogs could grin, this dog would have been grinning.

As far as he was concerned, he had found what he had been looking for all his life.

A family.

* * * * *

The road from Pine Gap Raceway to Greeneville Airport wound through the foothills of Rockcastle Mountain, then across a wide valley studded with neat little farms.

Hotshoe's Chevy was a classic. The engine throbbed with power. The mufflers were just barely legal.

"This was your ma's part of the world," Hotshoe said to Kin as the sleek little Chevy snaked through the turns on the narrow mountain roads. "You kids are all rooted here, even if you've never been here before. The mountains are in your blood, and blood's thicker than water."

"Sounds right to me," said Kin. He liked looking out the window at the houses tucked back in the hollows between the hills. Each house came with a barn. Sometimes he saw a horse or a cow. Sometimes he saw people tending their animals or working in small fields of bright green tobacco.

Some rode in endless circles on riding mowers, trimming lawns as big as hayfields.

"Lots of farmers can't stand retirement," Hotshoe said with a laugh. "They've got nothing else to do, so they buy themselves a toy tractor and keep driving in circles!"

Kin watched the world streak by the window and wondered what his life would be like if his mother had never left East Tennessee. Would he be happier if he had never seen a big city?

Or would he never have existed? Would some other boy, slightly different, be taking up his place in the world—some boy to whom the hills of Tennessee were the whole world?

"How come we're picking up Laura and Laptop?" Kin asked. "I thought they were going to stay with Aunt Adrian all summer."

"I thought so, too," said Hotshoe. "Then I got a call this morning."

"From Aunt Adrian?"

"It was from that weird husband of hers."

"Uncle Smedley."

"Right," said Hotshoe. "I don't mean to be talking down your family, but me and him always had even less to say to one another than me and your Aunt

Adrian. And me and your Aunt Adrian don't talk all that much, if you know what I mean."

"Anyway—" said Kin.

"Anyway, they are off for Paris in a hurry," Hotshoe explained. "They said they couldn't take the little ones with them on such short notice, on account of passports and visas and such, so I said fine, send them on down to Tennessee. They can travel with you and me on the NASCAR racing circuit for a while."

"Are you sure?" Kin asked. "Mama always said you didn't like to have little ones around."

As soon as Kin said it, he regretted it. Hotshoe looked hurt.

"She was remembering her own childhood," said Hotshoe after a moment's reflection. "It's true, I wasn't much of a dad. I kind of hope to make a better grandfather. People change, you know?"

"Sure," said Kin. "I guess." He reached for the knob on the dash. "Can I turn the radio on?"

Hotshoe smiled. "You can give it a try."

Kin turned the knob, but all he got was static. He tried all the way across the dial. Then he understood.

"It's only AM! There's no FM."

"Except for the engine, the four-speed tranny, and the mufflers, this car is stock," said Hotshoe. "All the way down to the radio dial. They didn't hardly have FM back in '55."

He shifted down to pass a slow-moving pickup on a hill. The little Chevy engine snarled with eager power.

"Besides," Hotshoe said, "who needs a radio when a small block Chevy V-8 makes such beautiful music?"

Greeneville Airport was in a narrow valley between two steep mountains. Private planes buzzed in and out, and a small jetliner from Atlanta or Cincinnati landed every hour or so.

Hotshoe found a parking place, and they hurried to the terminal. There were only two gates for arrivals and departures. Nobody seemed to mind a small yellow dog.

"We're just in time!" Hotshoe said.

The Appalachian flight from Atlanta was just pulling up to Gate One.

Kin couldn't believe how small the airport was. Only two gates!

Outside the big window, instead of a city he saw green fields and steep wooded hills. As he watched, a sleek private plane swooped down and landed on the runway, as light and graceful as a dancer.

"Worf!" said the dog.

"A Lear Jet," said Hotshoe, who loved all types of machinery. "Wonder what it's doing here?"

Just then the jetway opened and the first passengers started coming through Gate One. Kin was surprised to find himself looking forward to seeing his little brother and sister. He was tired of being the only Travis kid around.

"There's Laura!" Kin said.

He waved, and looked behind her for Laptop, who would be clutching his laptop computer, he knew.

But no, Laura was carrying the computer. She was walking slowly, looking down at her feet.

"She looks just like her mother when she was a kid," said Hotshoe. "But why does she look so sad?"

Something was wrong.

Laura—who was not much of a crier—was crying.

"Honey, what's the matter?" Hotshoe asked as he took Laura in his rugged arms. "What's the problem? And where's little Laptop?"

"He's gone!" Laura sobbed. "I lost him!"

LIKE A MOVIE STAR!

"Lost him!?" Kin said, astonished. "How can you lose an eight-year-old boy?"

"Laptop and I got on the plane together," said Laura, "and then I fell asleep before we even took off, and when I woke up—he was gone and we were in the air!"

"Don't tell me he fell out of the plane!" Hotshoe exclaimed.

"Not possible," said Kin, who watched the passengers streaming through the jetway as if he expected his little brother to be among them. Outside, he saw the sleek Lear Jet pulling up to the jetway at Gate Two.

"I don't know what happened!" wailed Laura. "It's another Travis family air disaster. First Mom and Dad, and now . . ."

"Can I help?" asked a strange voice.

It was a concerned-looking woman wearing an Appalachian Airlines uniform.

"I'm the flight attendant. I feel it was partly my fault."

"How's that?" Hotshoe asked, giving her a grim look.

The flight attendant put her arm around Laura's shoulder. "As I explained to Laura, I must have taken my eye off the jetway for a moment."

"Laptop was going to use the bathroom," said Laura. "He must not have known there was one on the plane."

"He must have slipped by me," said the flight attendant.

"That kid can slip by anybody!" said Kin.

"And so I closed the jetway and locked him out," said the flight attendant. "It wasn't Laura's fault."

"That means he's still at the Atlanta airport," said Hotshoe. "Let's call Lost and Found."

"I've already done that," said the flight attendant. "The pilot called from the air, and we got a negative."

"A negative?" Kin asked.

"They'd never heard of him. There are no lost kids at the Atlanta airport."

"He's dead, I just *know* he is!" Laura wailed.

"He has to be somewhere!" said Hotshoe, looking around the tiny terminal. "Maybe he wandered off."

"He *is* a little spacey," said Kin. "All he cares about is that computer of his."

"What if he's been kidnapped—or worse?" Laura wailed.

Just then they heard a familiar voice: "Laura! Kin!"

"Worf!" said the little yellow dog.

Kin and Laura both turned and saw their little brother hurrying out the jetway to Gate Two.

Behind him was a handsome young man in a leather jacket, brightly decorated with NASCAR racing colors.

"Jeff Gordon?!" Hotshoe said, puzzled.

It was, indeed, Jeff Gordon! While Laptop hugged his big brother and sister, the NASCAR superstar explained what had happened.

"I saw this kid looking lost in the lounge area," he said. "I was just getting ready to board my plane—"

"Of course!" Hotshoe broke in. "That was Jeff's Lear Jet we saw!"

"I thought maybe I should ask him if I could help out," said Jeff. "Then I figured it wasn't my business. Then while I was figuring out if I should speak to the kid, he came over and spoke to me. He asked if I was a race car driver."

"I could tell by his outfit," said Laptop.

Jeff Gordon laughed. He held out his arms, which were covered with bright patches. "I said, 'Either I am or I'm a serious wannabe.'"

Laura looked amazed. "You've never been to a stock car race, Laptop. So how'd you know what a race driver looks like?"

Laptop looked insulted. "NASCAR has a cool Web site," he said.

"I'm wearing my racing colors," Jeff said, "since I just came from a personal appearance in Atlanta. And I wanted to hurry up to Pine Gap Raceway so I could get in a little practice."

"I asked him if he knew you, Grandpa," Laptop said.

"I said, 'Who doesn't?'" laughed Jeff Gordon. "Hotshoe Hunter is a legend."

Hotshoe blushed. "You make me sound dead."

"Well, you're not racing anymore," said Jeff. "And that's good for us younger guys. Anyway, Larry here told me his story and I knew he was stuck. So to make a long story short, I was heading the same way, so here we are."

"You should see the inside of his Lear Jet!" said Larry. "It's totally radical."

"I don't know how to thank you," said Hotshoe.

"No need," said Jeff with a grin. "I'm sure you would have done the same for me. We're all one big family here," he said to the kids.

"In that case—" Laura stuck out her hand. "I'm Laura, Mr. Gordon."

"Jeff."

"Jeff, then. And I want to thank you for saving my little brother's life, not to mention my reputation as a baby-sitter."

"You're no baby-sitter, 'cause I'm no baby!" protested Laptop, grabbing the computer out of her hand. "And give me my computer, anyway!"

"Very pleased to meet you, Laura," said Jeff Gordon.

"Let us give you a ride to the track," said Hotshoe.

"Love to," said Jeff. "But I need to rent a car. I'll see you folks tomorrow at the time trials."

He shook hands with Laptop, waved good-bye to the others, and he was gone toward the car rental counter. The flight attendant waved and was gone in the opposite direction.

"What a cute dog," said Laura, looking down. "What's his name?"

"He doesn't have a name yet," said Kin.

"A dog has to have a name," said Laptop.

"Worf!" said the little yellow dog.

"Well, kids, all's well that ends well," said Hotshoe as they picked up the bags and started toward the car. "But I don't ever want you pulling a stunt like that again, Laptop. You scared your sister to death."

- - - - - - - - - - - - - - -

"Yessir," said Laptop.

"I think she's still in a coma," said Kin.

Laura was staring off into space with a dizzy smile on her face.

"What's the matter, honey?" asked Hotshoe. "Are you okay?"

"I think I know what it is," said Kin. "It's that Jeff Gordon fellow, isn't it?"

"He looks like a movie star," sighed Laura.

"He's a superstar," said Hotshoe. "He's just about the best and most famous stock car driver around."

"He said he was glad you weren't driving," said Kin.

"Does that mean the old-timers like yourself were better?"

"Naw!" said Hotshoe. "He was just being polite. His generation is way ahead of where we were. They're more scientific, better trained as athletes. Better all-round drivers."

* * * * *

"I'm hungry!" said Laptop.

"We'll get something to eat," said Hotshoe as they picked up the bags and headed out toward the parking lot.

"You're always hungry," said Kin. He gave his little brother a swat. Just to prove he was glad to see him.

Sort of.

"Stop that!" complained Laptop. But he smiled, just to let his big brother know he was glad to see him.

Sort of.

Laura was still gazing dreamily into space.

"Earth to Laura," said Kin.

"I thought all race drivers were—you know . . ." Laura stammered.

"Ugly old grease monkeys like me?" Hotshoe laughed. "Some of us are. But the Good Lord in his infinite wisdom threw in a few young lookers like Jeff just to keep things interesting to all you young girls."

"Can I drive?" asked Kin when they got to the parking lot. The '55 Chevy gleamed in the sun.

"Do you have a license?" Hotshoe asked.

"No. Not yet."

"Well, then," said Hotshoe as he unlocked the door on the driver's side and got in, "You just answered your own question, didn't you? Now, you kids get in and let's go get some dinner. I have a lot of work to do tonight. Everybody is still experimenting with camshaft profiles, and time trials are tomorrow, you know!"

The Chevy started with a beautiful mellow roar, and soon they were on the road, heading for the track.

"There's a chicken place!" said Laptop.

"There's a seafood place!" said Laura.

"There's a pizza place!" said Kin.

"Worf!" said the little yellow dog as the Chevy passed a pet food store.

"I've got a better idea," said Hotshoe, stepping on the gas and roaring past the row of fast-food restaurants. "The track."

"The race track?" Larry asked.

"That's the only place you can get real old-fashioned Southern cooking anymore," said Hotshoe.

"We're going to eat at the race track?" Laura asked. Her lip curled up with disgust.

"The best little restaurant in seven states," said Hotshoe. "A little place called Infield Annie's."

SHADE TREE MECHANICS

It was dark by the time Hotshoe's '55 Chevy, with its load of hungry kids and one hungry dog, got to the Pine Gap Raceway.

"That's got to be the ugliest dog I ever saw," said Hotshoe as they walked across the infield.

"Don't talk that way in front of him," said Kin. "You'll hurt his feelings."

"He doesn't understand," said Laura.

"He's pretty smart," said Kin.

Laptop shook his head. "Computers are smart," he said. "Dogs are just cute."

Laura shook her head. "Cats are cute," she said. "Dogs are—I don't know. What are they?"

"Worf!" said the little dog with no name.

"Faithful," said Kin. "He just said, 'Dogs are faithful.'"

"Don't tell me you can understand him!" said Laura.

"Worf," said Kin with a sly smile.

The garage area was lighted and bustling with mechanics and technicians hard at work. But the pits, the track, and the infield were deserted.

Even Infield Annie's was dark and looked closed. But when Hotshoe and his grandchildren reached the mobile outdoor kitchen, they found Annie cleaning up.

"Well, if it ain't Hotshoe!" she said. "You're just in time for leftovers. And who are these shady-looking characters?"

"My grandchildren," said Hotshoe. "Laura, Laptop, and McKinley—meet my oldest and best friend, Infield Annie."

"I'm not all that old," said Annie. She squinted at Kin. "One of these I know already," she said, shaking Kin's hand. "Why didn't you tell me you were Hotshoe Hunter's grandson?"

"I uh—I didn't know you knew him," said Kin.

"Everybody knows Hotshoe," said Annie. "You kids sit down and I'll serve you some dinner."

"Where's the menu?" asked Laptop.

"Menu? Boy, are you in for a surprise!" said Kin.

Soon all three kids were sitting at one of Annie's folding tables, enjoying a meal of corn bread and beans.

"I wanted a hot dog," said Laptop. "How come we didn't get what we ordered?"

"'Cause that's the way Annie is," said Kin. "Besides, this food is pretty good, huh?"

"Not if you ask me," said Laptop.

"This is real Southern cooking," said Hotshoe. "These beans are what make race cars go fast."

"Watch your mouth, old man," said Annie. "And I want you kids to know—you can order anything you want at Infield Annie's."

"And you'll always get what she wants you to have," said Kin.

Laura didn't mind. She liked Annie. She liked her big red hands and warm motherly ways. Plus, she liked the corn bread and beans.

At least that's something Southern that's not terrible, she thought to herself.

While the kids ate, Annie pulled Hotshoe aside.

"That's a fine-looking mess of grandchildren you've got there," she said. "They're poor Clara's, I guess, God rest her soul."

"Yep," said Hotshoe, wiping a tear from his eye. "Hers and Tom's. And they're pretty good kids, seems like."

"Well, I hope you make a better grandfather than you were a father," Annie said.

Hotshoe blushed. "I'm trying my best. I'm sharing custody with their Aunt Adrian."

"I didn't know you had two daughters."

"I didn't," said Hotshoe. "Clara was my one and only. Adrian is their father's sister. I have actually never met her. But according to Clara and Tom's will, the custody is to be split between me and her. I guess we'll have to meet sometime."

"Aunt Adrian lives in a *huge* house," said Laptop.

"Quit bragging," said Laura.

"I'm not bragging," said Laptop.

"Yes you are," said Kin.

"Am not!" said Laptop.

"You kids hush and eat your dinner," said Hotshoe. "The fact is," he said to Annie, "Adrian does have a lot of money. She and Tom were from one of those fine old New England families."

"Hmmmph," snorted Annie, who didn't think much of high society. "Clara was from a fine old family, too. Yours."

"Aw, shucks," said Hotshoe. "Us Hunters are just a bunch of dirt farmers and shade tree mechanics."

"What's a shade tree mechanic?" Laptop asked. "I thought shade trees didn't have any parts to fix or replace."

Annie and Hotshoe both laughed.

"It's an old Southern expression," said Hotshoe. "It means a mechanic who doesn't even have a garage, just works out under a tree."

"Not like NASCAR," said Kin.

"Not these days," said Hotshoe. "But in the early days, stock car racing was pretty low to the ground.

NASCAR was a bunch of good old boys like Junior Johnson—men who could fix a car with their eyes closed, and could drive the pants off anybody that dared to chase them."

"Like revenuers," said Annie.

"True enough," said Hotshoe. "I learned to drive running moonshine myself. It seemed almost respectable in those days. We took to hopping up cars to get away from the law."

"Then they decided to get together on Saturday night and see who could drive the fastest," said Annie. "And it all kind of took off from there."

"More and more folks showed up to watch. They took to cheering on their favorite drivers," said Hotshoe. "Then somebody got the idea of building a real race track and charging admission."

"And selling food," said Annie.

"Cars going in circles!" said Laura with a sneer. "Sounds boring to me."

"You'd be surprised, honey," said Annie. "You might even grow to like it."

"I doubt it," said Laura.

"Well, I have work to do," said Hotshoe. "Several camshaft replacements tonight. Qualifying runs are tomorrow. You kids can hang out in the RV and watch TV."

"What are qualifying runs?" asked Laptop.

"Same thing as time trials," said Kin.

"That's no help!" said Laptop.

"You'll see tomorrow," said Hotshoe. "It'll all become clear."

"Worf!" said the little dog.

"Laura, will you walk with me back to my trailer?" Annie asked. "Let the menfolk go on ahead, I have something to show you."

GIRL TALK

Laura and Laptop had already dropped off their luggage in Hotshoe's RV, which was parked in the infield, next to the garage.

Annie's Airstream trailer was parked right beside it. It was all metal, and as sleek as a bullet.

"Cool," said Laptop as they walked past. "It looks like a rocket ship. Can I see inside?"

"Tomorrow," said Annie. "You boys go on over to Hotshoe's and watch TV. I want to have a little girl talk with your sister."

"Girl talk, what's that?" said Laptop.

"None of your business," said Kin, grabbing his brother's hand and dragging him off.

* * * * *

"Girl talk?" Laura asked.

"Nothing serious," said Annie. "I just wanted to get rid of those two."

Annie opened the door to the trailer and Laura stepped in.

"Wow! It's—beautiful!" she said.

The inside of Annie's trailer was a patchwork of bright colors. The curved walls were covered with handmade quilts, and the floor was covered with handmade hooked rugs.

"I collect American crafts," said Annie. "They fit in with the spirit of racing. They're another part of Americana."

"I love it here," said Laura, sitting on the sofa. "My mother collected stuff like this."

"Clara did? I'll bet you miss her," said Annie.

Laura nodded, not trusting her voice. "You knew her?"

"Yep. I was a good friend of your grandpa, especially after his wife died. I loved your mom when she was a little girl. I taught her how to play the guitar."

"She was a piano teacher. I never knew she played guitar," said Laura.

"She quit guitar when she ran away up North,"

Annie said. "Your granddad was too strict on her, and she wanted to see the big world. She went up North to college and never looked back. It kinda broke your granddaddy's heart."

"Wow," said Laura. "Did she break your heart, too?"

"Only a little," said Annie. "Besides, that's what hearts are for. Just like kids are made to grow up and become independent, and birds are made to fly. She was quite a girl. Real musical, too. Do you play?"

"I'm learning the piano," Laura said. "Or at least I was, before we got shipped here for the summer."

"Well, your mother left something behind, which I promised to keep for her just in case she ever came back to get it."

Annie reached into a narrow closet and pulled out a black guitar case. Inside was a small steel-string flat-top guitar, inlaid with mother-of-pearl.

"It's beautiful!" said Laura.

It was indeed beautiful. "It was your mother's," said Annie. "She could play it, too. She used to play at my place and bring in a real crowd. Go ahead, pick it up. Hold it. It's yours."

Laura picked up the guitar and curled the fingers of her left hand around the strings. They seemed to know just where to go.

With her right hand, she struck a chord.

Then another. Her left hand seemed to find the strings; her right hand brushed the chords.

The music filled the little trailer.

"Wow," said Annie. "You should have told me you know how to play guitar!"

"That's just it," said Laura, looking down at her fingers in amazement. "I can't! I've never held a guitar in my life, much less played one."

The boys were watching TV when Laura got to her grandfather's RV.

Laura set the guitar case on the floor.

"Wow," said Laptop. "What's in there?"

"What do you think?" said Kin. "A machine gun!"

"It's a guitar, and it belonged to Mother," said Laura. "But now it's mine."

"Just because you're a girl?" Kin protested. "That's not fair."

"Can I hold it?" Laptop was already opening the case. "Where do you plug it in?"

"You don't," said Laura. "It's acoustic."

"Bo-ring!" said Laptop, closing the case and turning back to his computer.

"It's pretty," said Kin. "Did Mama really play this guitar?"

"According to Annie, she was pretty good," said Laura.

"Are you going to learn?"

"Well, that's just it," said Laura. "Watch this."

She picked up the guitar and struck a chord.

Both her brothers watched in stunned amazement.

"When did you learn to play the guitar?" Kin asked.

"I didn't," said Laura. "It's almost like the guitar is playing me. But I don't understand how it could be."

"I understand it," said Laptop. "It's magic."

FIND A FRIEND

Laptop opened his eyes and looked around the unfamiliar, tiny room.

He reached up and touched the ceiling.

He reached out and touched the wall.

He was in a box!

Then he remembered: He was in his grandpa's RV.

Laptop was in the tiny alcove over the driver's seat. He leaned out and looked down. His brother Kin was snoring away on the fold-out couch.

Laura had been given the only bedroom, in the back. ("Why do girls always get everything?" Kin and Laptop had both complained.)

Laptop pulled his Apricot 07 laptop computer out from under his pillow. It was his best friend.

He climbed down out of his little loft. The RV's

combination living room, dining room, and kitchen was about the size of a bathroom in Aunt Adrian's house in Boston.

Grandpa Hotshoe had left a note:

"Kids: I'm at the garage if you need me. Annie sent over some biscuits, and there's milk in the fridge. HS."

Laptop grabbed a biscuit and poured himself a glass of milk.

"Worf," said a small voice. It was the little yellow dog. Laptop had forgotten him.

"Oh, it's you," he said, pouring the dog a bowl of milk and setting it beside a biscuit on the floor.

The RV was a mess. There were a few dusty trophies, wired to a narrow shelf so they wouldn't fall when the RV was on the road. Beside them was a picture of Hotshoe as a young man, wearing a racing uniform and holding a helmet. He was standing next to a big, old-fashioned car. Beside him was a beautiful woman with honey-blond hair who looked a lot like Laptop's mom.

The woman had a baby in her arms.

Must be Mom, Laptop thought. It was hard to imagine his mother had once been a baby. It was even harder to imagine that she was gone.

Laptop squeezed his eyes shut and counted to ten. That was his way of pushing sad thoughts out of his head.

Laptop opened his eyes again. Sunlight streamed in the narrow window. It was a bright, sunny day, but he didn't feel like going outside. What was there to do?

The distant roar of an engine reminded him that he was at the race track. Big deal. Cars were bo-ring. Race cars didn't even have computer chips.

He ate his cereal and then opened his Apricot 07. It was the last computer his father had worked on before the plane crash.

It was hooked up to the Internet through a remote cellular modem connection. Laptop checked his e-mail every morning. He had "e-mail pals" around the world.

The computer was always booted up, but it "went

to sleep" when he wasn't using it. He hit a key to "wake it up."

A chime rang, and a box popped up on the screen: "You have mail."

Most of it was familiar: jokes, greetings, "spam," stupid chain letters. But there was one mysterious message, from someone called GW at spirit.com.

Laptop clicked on it.

"GO OUTSIDE AND MAKE A FRIEND."

Spirit.com?

GW? Guess Who?

Laptop looked suspiciously toward his brother or sister. Had one of them been tampering with his machine?

It didn't matter. Taking a walk wasn't a bad idea. There was nothing else to do anyway. He put his computer back to sleep, pulled on his shoes, and stuck a biscuit in his pocket for later.

"Worf?" asked a tiny voice.

The little yellow dog was waiting patiently by the door.

"Sure," Laptop said. "You can come."

- - - - - - - - - - - - - - - -

It was only eight A.M. The infield was empty, even though the garage was already bustling with activity. The roar of an engine from the garage reminded Laptop that he was at the race track.

Engines, he thought. *Cars. Bo-ring*!

"Come on!" he hollered.

With the dog following, he broke into a run. He headed toward the center of the infield, where the grass was high.

Laptop ran faster and faster. It felt good to stretch his legs and streak through the high grass. It got higher and higher, until it reached his waist, then his shoulders.

"Whoa!" Suddenly Laptop skidded to a stop. He had almost run into a pond.

The little yellow dog slid to a stop beside him, tumbling end over end.

"Your feet are too big for your legs," said Laptop, picking him up. "I guess that's just because you're just a puppy."

Then he caught himself and said, "*Just* a puppy. I sound like a grown-up! I know how you feel. Everybody ranking on you all the time, just because you're small."

"Worf," said the little dog.

"You can say that again," said Laptop.

"Worf."

The pond was in the exact center of the infield, hidden from the outside world by the weeds. It was muddy and round and only about twenty feet across. But it looked deep.

The little dog crept to the edge. He put one paw into the muddy water, then another.

"Worf!" he said, and jumped back.

Laptop leaned over and looked down. Something was in there, moving around.

Something big.

Then it was gone. Or had it been his imagination?

"It wasn't your imagination," said a strange voice. "There's something down there, all right."

Laptop jumped and looked behind him.

There was no one there.

"Huh?" Laptop said.

"It's a big old catfish," said a voice in a thick

Southern accent. "We call him Moby Cat. He'll eat any-thing, but he especially loves tender little dogs."

The little dog shivered.

"Moby who?" asked Laptop. "And who are you? Where are you? I can't see anybody."

"Look closer," said the voice. "Look down."

Laptop stared at the muddy ground. He saw the shadow of a man standing by the pond. The problem was, there was no man—just the shadow.

The shadow waved. "See me now?"

"I can see your shadow," said Laptop. "But that's all."

"I can fix that," said the shadow. "Got anything to eat?"

Laptop pulled the crumbling biscuit out of his pocket.

"Smells good!" The shadow waved an arm, and to Laptop's amazement, a cloud appeared in the cloud-less sky.

It covered the sun and the shadow went away.

In its place stood a man in a ragged and tattered Civil War uniform.

A RACE TRACK GHOST

"You Yankees sure talk funny," said the soldier in a slight Southern drawl.

"How do you know I'm a Yankee?" asked Laptop.

"I wasn't born yesterday," said the man. "Not by a long shot." He looked about thirty-five years old. He wore wool pants and a dirty coat with threadbare gold braid. The pants and coat were so worn and dirty that they could have been either gray or blue. His brass belt buckle had three letters on it. The first letter was hard to read, but the second two were "SA." His shaggy brown hair looked like it hadn't been cut in a long time.

"Here." Laptop held out the biscuit, but the soldier shook his head.

"I can't eat that," he said. "I just wanted to smell it."

He no longer cast a shadow at all. But neither did Laptop, now that the sun was behind a cloud.

"I was expecting you," the soldier said. He sat down on the grass and crossed his legs. "I even know your name. It's Laptop. You future folks sure have funny names."

"What do you mean, *future*? Are you from the past?"

"We're all from the past," said the soldier. "Heading for the future but never quite getting there."

"How do you know my name, anyway?" Laptop asked, amazed. But was that any more amazing than a Civil War soldier appearing out of thin air?

"Let's just say I'm a friend of a friend. My name's Delbert but you can call me Dell. What's the dog's name?"

"He doesn't have a name."

"A dog has to have a name."

"Worf!" said the little yellow dog.

"See?" said Dell. He smiled. "Most dogs can't see me. Only cats, mostly. Mind if I pet him?"

"Go ahead," said Laptop. "He's not my dog anyway. We're just friends."

The soldier ran his hand along the dog's back. Laptop noticed that the hair on the dog's back didn't move when the soldier's hand touched it. But the dog seemed to like it.

"Worf," he said softly.

"You here for the races?" Laptop asked.

"Heck no!" Dell sneered. "I don't hold with racing. What's the hurry? Time goes on forever, you know. And it goes in a circle, too."

Delbert, or Dell, looked kind of dim. Larry could almost see through him. If he stared real hard, he could see weeds behind the soldier, as if he were a dirty window and not a real, solid human being.

"Are you a ghost?" Laptop asked. "A Civil War ghost?"

"Was I killed in the war? Yep. That's about the size of it."

"So where's your gun?"

"Got rid of it. Buried it. Broke it. Threw it away.

- - - - - - - - - - - - - - - - -

Tossed it. Finito. Fini. Gone."

"Why?"

"If you'd ever been in a war, you'd know."

"Which side were you on? Union or Confederate?"

"I don't remember," said Dell. "All I remember is fighting and marching. And then getting killed, I guess."

"You talk like you're from the South," said Laptop. "That must mean you're a Confederate."

"Not exactly," said Dell. "I'm from Kentucky, and Kentuckians fought on both sides. Lots of folks from here in East Tennessee fought for the Union, too."

"I can't tell if your uniform is gray or blue," said Laptop. "Maybe your belt buckle will say."

"I thought of that." The soldier looked down at his belt. "The first letter was hit by a bullet, though. Could be either a C or a U. CSA or USA. Could be either one."

"That must be weird," said Laptop. "Not to know what you died for."

"It is," said Dell. "But being a ghost in general is weird."

"I never heard of a ghost in the daytime," said Laptop. "I don't really believe in ghosts, anyway. Nothing personal."

"I didn't believe either, until I became one," said Dell. "Luckily, what I *believe* and what *happens* are two different things."

"So why are you here?" asked Laptop. "Was this a Civil War battlefield?"

"You might say that. The entire South was a Civil War battlefield," said Dell. "Folks that weren't fighting the Yankees were fighting one another. Lots of folks died."

"My parents died," said Laptop. "But it was a plane crash, not a war."

"I know, and I'm sorry," said Dell. "For you, that is. Not so much for them. Death isn't all that bad. It's just different."

"Different from what?"

"Different from life, what do you think? For example, you don't stop caring about your kids after you're dead. But you don't have any way of showing it. Sometimes you do it in funny ways."

Laptop looked up. He got a strange feeling. "You mean—like—my parents might have talked to you?"

Dell shrugged. "Could be. I can't exactly say. I'm not allowed to reveal Death's secrets. Let's just say here I am, and leave it at that."

"Whatever."

"Laptop! There you are!"

Laptop turned around and saw his big brother Kin crashing through the weeds.

"There you are!" Kin said again. "What're you doing? Come on, let's watch the time trials."

"Wait," said Laptop. "I want you to meet somebody . . ."

But the Civil War soldier was gone. The sun had come out, and all that was left was his shadow.

Then even the shadow was gone.

"Where'd he go?" Laptop asked.

"Worf!" said the little dog.

"Where'd who go?" Kin asked.

"The stranger. A friend," Laptop explained. "There was a guy sitting here. On the grass. A Civil War soldier."

- - - - - - - - - - - - - - -

"Sure," said Kin, rolling his eyes. "Happens all the time. Union or Confederate?"

"He couldn't remember," said Laptop. "But he was definitely a Civil War ghost. I was talking to him."

"Yeah, sure, and I'm the Hunchback of Notre Dame," said Kin. "Come on, we don't have time for fantasy games. Time trials are starting soon. I told Grandpa Hotshoe I would look after you."

"I don't need anybody to look after me," said Laptop. But he followed his big brother out of the weeds, toward the race track.

THE WING THINGY

"I saw you had your mother's old guitar out last night," said Hotshoe. He had come back to the RV to check on the kids. Kin and Laptop were already out, and Laura was alone.

"Annie gave it to me," said Laura, finishing her breakfast biscuit.

"I didn't know you knew how to play."

"I don't. That is, I didn't. That is, I didn't think I did either," said Laura. "But something happened when I put my fingers on the strings."

She told her grandfather about how her fingers had found the chords.

"It was like somebody else was playing with me."

"Maybe somebody was," Hotshoe said.

"Like who?"

Hotshoe looked away, his eyes glistening. "I don't know," he said. "Let's you and me head down to the garage and see what's up."

The grandstand and the infield were filling up with racing fans.

They brought coolers filled with picnic lunches, lotion to protect against the sun, ponchos for sudden showers, and banners to show support for their favorite drivers.

GO JEFF! read one banner.

GO TEXAS TERRY! read another.

Hotshoe and Laura were crossing the infield toward the garage. Hotshoe was wearing his Merlin MixMaster jacket and hat.

"I thought the race was tomorrow," said Laura. "Why are all these people arriving today?"

"To watch qualifying," said Hotshoe. "The cars race one at a time, against the clock. The fastest car gets the best spot for the start, the inside lane in the front. It's called the pole position, because that's where the checkered flag used to hang from the pole."

"That's weird," said Laura. "It seems like the fastest car should start in the back, to make it more fair."

"Then he would have to run over everybody right away," said Hotshoe. "Racing isn't handicapped. NASCAR has the same rules for every car and driver."

He looked at his watch.

"Hey, I'm running late! Laura, if you don't mind hanging out with an old man, you're welcome to come with me to the garage."

"Love to," said Laura.

As Laura followed her grandfather through the growing infield crowd toward the garage, she was surprised by what she saw. She had expected stock car racing fans to be all guys—beer-bellied, loud-talking rednecks.

Instead, she saw every type of person—black and white, young and old, men and women.

She had expected them to all be dressed in coveralls and clodhoppers, like the Beverly Hillbillies.

A few were—but many more were not. The

women were as sophisticated and as well dressed as the women in Boston.

The boys looked, well, cool. Most of them, anyway.

"Penny for your thoughts," said Hotshoe.

"Huh?"

"It's an old expression. It means, what are you thinking about so hard?"

"Oh, nothing," said Laura. "I was just thinking how people down South here don't look all that different from people up North."

"Just a little better looking, honey, that's all," said her grandfather with a twinkle in his eye.

"I don't get it," Laura said a few minutes later, when they were walking through the garage, watching the mechanics and crews ready the bright colorful cars for the time trials.

"Don't get what?" asked Hotshoe.

"Stock. Doesn't *stock* mean normal, or standard?"

"Yes."

"So why are these race cars called stock cars?" Laura asked. "They're called stock cars, but they aren't normal. And it's not just because they are all painted up like crazy. They don't have headlights, or glove compartments, or even doors like normal cars."

"You're right," Hotshoe laughed. "There's very little stock about a stock car. They *look* like the regular cars you see on the street, but that's about it. The engines, the bodies, even the frames are specially built."

"Then why call them stock cars?" Laura asked.

"Well, that's a good question," said Hotshoe. "Back when I was racing, they *were* stock. Mostly, anyway. You'd take a Ford or a Plymouth or a Chevy and hop it up a little, and you were in business. Maybe heavier wheels, better brakes, but that was all. That's why the fans came. People liked seeing something that looked like the car in their own driveway, or on their local dealer's lot.

"I see," said Laura.

"The idea was, folks would watch 'em race on Saturday or Sunday and buy one on Monday. The big car companies supported racing teams. But these days only a few parts of the car are stock. A Pontiac, like that one there—"

He pointed at a race car being wheeled out of the garage onto the track.

"That's my client Steve Gregson's car. I just put in a new camshaft for him. See how his car's shaped exactly like a Pontiac Grand Prix? But the body, like the frame, is super-slick and specially built for racing."

"I see. And what's that little wing thingy on the back?" Laura asked.

"That 'wing thingy,' as you call it, is the spoiler," Hotshoe laughed.

"*Spoiler?*" Laura was shocked. "Why spoil things?"

"It keeps the car on the ground," said Hotshoe. "At 190 mph, the rear end wants to float unless you use the wind to press it down."

"I see," said Laura. And she did—almost, anyway. She was almost even having a good time, in spite of herself. There was something about the colorful cars and the shimmering air that said *summer*. Even the sharp smell of gasoline was growing familiar. And that Jeff Gordon sure was cute!

Maybe the South wouldn't be so bad after all!

IN THE PITS

Laptop wanted to name the dog Chip. "A dog has to have a name!" he said. "Isn't that right—Chip?"

The little yellow dog was silent.

"See?" said Kin. "It has to be the right name. Not just any name. Chip is a stupid name. It's almost as stupid as Spot or Fido."

"It is not!" said Laptop. "And even if it is, how will we know when we find the right name?"

"What do you mean, *we*?" asked Kin. "He's my dog."

"He is not, he's *our* dog!" said Laptop. "Aren't you?"

"Worf worf!" said the little yellow dog with no name.

Kin and Laptop left the RV and walked across the infield toward the fence to watch the time trials.

The little dog followed.

Laptop was trying to convince Kin he had seen a

ghost. "His name was Dell," he said. "He was dressed like a Civil War soldier, honest! Except you couldn't tell which kind. I think he was killed here."

"According to Grandpa Hotshoe, the race track was once part of a Civil War battlefield," said Kin. "But there are probably legends like that all around this area. You know darn well that there's no such thing as ghosts. And you know what Mom and Dad said about lying."

"What did they say about lying?"

"They said only liars do it. Now, let's hurry. I want to get a good spot to watch the cars qualify."

"Whatever," said Laptop. He clutched his computer to his side and followed his big brother.

There was no point in arguing with grown-ups.

And Kin was acting more and more like a grown-up these days.

It was disgusting!

The boys were almost at the fence when Kin felt a hand on his arm.

"Hey, hoss!"

- - - - - - - - - - - - - - - - -

It was Junior Peytona. He was decked out in Peytona Racing Team colors.

"Hi, Junior," said Kin. He introduced his little brother to his new friend.

"You can call me Laptop," said Larry.

"I can see why," said Junior, nodding toward the computer tucked under the boy's arm. "Why don't you two come with me and watch the time trials from the pits."

"Why not," said Kin.

"Worf!" said the little yellow dog.

"That dog have a name yet?" asked Junior, scratching the dog's ears.

The pits. It sounded exciting to Laptop, like a cave or a hideout.

He was disappointed to see that the pits were just parking spots on the inside of the race track.

The Waddy Peytona Racing Team pit was filled with busy crew members in colorful uniforms, preparing the blue and yellow Taurus for its qualifying run.

Junior introduced Laptop to the team's crew chief. He was a thin, red-haired man who walked bent over, as if he were always looking for something that had dropped on the ground.

"Copacetic," said the crew chief as he shook hands with Laptop. "You can just call me Cope. Everybody does."

"I can see why," said Laptop.

It was mid-morning before the time trials started.

From the pits, the cars sounded like angry bees as they roared around the banked turns at over 150 miles per hour.

Laptop watched from the pit wall as the cars ran, one at a time. Each car got a practice lap and a timed lap. The times were announced by the loudspeaker.

"Steve Gregson at 162.35."

"Terry Labonte, 161.34."

"Jeff Gordon, 162.07."

Laptop whispered "Yes!" Even in the Waddy Peytona pit, he felt like a Jeff Gordon fan.

"The Gray Brothers . . ." said the announcer in his big booming voice.

Junior and Kin watched, puzzled, as a strange car streaked past.

- - - - - - - - - - - - - - - - -

Most NASCAR race cars were a patchwork of bright ads, names, trademarks, and designs.

But not this one. It was dull gray, the color of a rain cloud.

"Looks like a stealth fighter," said Junior.

"Runs like one, too," said Waddy. "Looks like this is the car to beat tomorrow."

"Who are these Gray Brothers?" Cope asked.

"Beats me," said Waddy. "They never socialize with anybody. They just race. They never win but they never come in last. And I don't know where they go between races."

"A dog has to have a name," said Junior. "How about Spot?"

"Thanks, Junior. We're working on it," said Kin.

He was more interested in the activity in Waddy Peytona's pit, where air compressors, tools, extra parts, and big gas cans were neatly arranged for fast and easy access.

Two air wrenches for changing tires, both shaped like heavy pistols, stood like weapons waiting for the draw. A wheeled jack, itself as sleek as a race car, was rolled against the wall.

Waddy came back from the Officials' Booth, carrying his helmet. The crew gathered around him.

"We drew a late number," Waddy said. "We're qualifying after lunch." He looked worried.

"Is that bad?" Kin asked.

"On a sunny day like today, it is," said Cope. "The track gets hot in the afternoon, and it slows you down. It's better to run on cool tires and a cool track."

"We need a pole position bad," said Junior.

"That's right," said Waddy. "We need a new sponsor. Wabash Guitars is interested. They'll be in the stands today."

"If we can finish in the top qualifiers, it'll impress them for sure!" said Junior eagerly.

"And if we don't impress them, we're in trouble," said Waddy. "I can't afford to run without a sponsor."

"All we have to do is pray for clouds," said Cope, looking up at the sky.

His smile turned to a frown.

The sky was bright and clear.

Soon the team was hard at work, tuning the engine and getting the car ready to run.

"A dog has to have a name," said Tach.

"How about Fido?" said Carl.

"Thanks anyway," said Kin. "We're working on it."

"Tach, you and Carl take a break!" said Waddy. "Don't wear yourselves out. Remember, we have to swap engines tonight, after the qualifying runs."

"Swap engines?" Kin asked.

Junior nodded. "We have a new engine for the race," he said. "This qualifier has already run three races. It's broken in good."

"Why don't you race with it, then, if it's faster?"

"In a race, reliability is as important as speed," said Tach. "For the time trials, we can go all out. Notice the flat fan. That saves a little horsepower. We don't need to worry so much about cooling for the two or three qualifying laps."

"Why don't you just take the fan off?" Laptop asked.

"NASCAR regulations," said Cope. "There are a

heck of a lot of them. Mostly geared toward safety, but also toward keeping the competition alive."

"We run used tires, too," said Junior.

"Old tires?"

"Not old tires. Just tires that have been around the track a time or two. The tread has been scuffed a little. That makes them slightly faster for the time trials."

"It's all just tricks of the trade," said Cope. "Junior, you better get to work and put those scuffs on. Maybe your friend Kin there can help you."

Junior pulled two slightly worn tires from the pile and carried them to the car, one at a time. "Help me put on these scuffs," he said to Kin.

"These what?"

"Scuffs. That's what we call used tires."

"That's it!" said Laptop and Kin, both at the same time.

"That's what?" asked Junior.

"The name!" said Kin.

"For the dog!" said Laptop.

"Worf worf!" said Scuffs, happy to finally have a name.

MUSIC IS MAGIC

"The pits are the areas on the inside of the track where the cars pull in to be refueled and get their tires changed during a race," Hotshoe explained to his granddaughter. "Each team has its own pit. NASCAR regulations specify how many crew members can be in each pit, and even how many tools. Only two air wrenches are allowed, for example."

"What do inspectors look for?" asked Laura.

"Everything," said Hotshoe. "NASCAR has a lot of rules, and that means there are lots of ways to . . . well, get creative."

"Stock car drivers are cheaters?" asked Laura, shocked. All the colorful characters she had met so far had seemed honest and upright.

"No, no, no, they're not!" said Hotshoe. "But they

are highly competitive, and everybody's looking for that little edge. In my day, it may have been nothing more than an oversized fuel line that would hold an extra lap or two between the tank and the engine. Or maybe a shaved front end that would give a car an extra half a mile per hour. These days it's mostly the little things they look for."

Little things indeed. Laura was amazed at how complicated racing could be.

On the track outside, the cars sounded like angry bees. The speeds were incredible, but each car was only a fraction of a second faster or slower than the one before.

After a while Laura got bored. She looked at the clock on the grandstand and saw that it was almost noon.

"I'm going on over to Infield Annie's for lunch," she told her grandfather.

"I'll come later," said Hotshoe. "I have a camshaft to check out."

There was a big line at Infield Annie's. Racing fans and crew members in bright colors talked eagerly about today's qualifying runs and tomorrow's race, as they waited patiently for Annie's famous Southern cooking.

Annie was behind the counter, filling drinks with one hand and serving food with the other. She moved so fast that her hands were just a blur. Each plate she served was topped with a golden buttermilk biscuit.

No matter what anyone ordered, every customer got the same. But no one was complaining. The picnic tables were already filled with people eating country ham, okra, and sweet potatoes.

"Can I help?" Laura asked, ducking under the counter. She couldn't believe how fast Annie's hands were moving.

"You sure can, honey," said Annie, hardly pausing as she filled plates and cups, passed out napkins, took money and made change in one complex motion. "Go over to Hotshoe's RV and get your guitar."

"But I can't play!" said Laura.

"That's not what I heard last night," said Annie.

"But that's just it," Laura whispered. "I don't know how I did it. It was like magic."

"Music *is* magic," said Annie. "And you are your mother's daughter. Don't question your talent, just accept it. Now run, child, hurry! I need somebody to help entertain this crowd. Otherwise, they'll all get restless.

"What's wrong with that?" Laura asked.

"Hush, girl, and get moving!"

Laura pulled the guitar out of the closet at her grandfather's RV and carried it back to Annie's.

Annie pointed at a spot on the counter, and Laura jumped up and sat down.

She struck the strings. The guitar sounded good. But was it in tune? How would she know?

"You'll know," said Annie, as if she were reading Laura's mind. "Just go with it. Trust your heart."

Laura closed her eyes and struck a chord. It was just like last night. Her fingers seemed to know exactly where to go, what strings to press, and what strings to pluck. They seemed to know what chord followed next, too.

Soon Laura was playing a song, even though she didn't know what it was.

When she finished, she heard scattered applause. She opened her eyes. The people in the line were watching her, and smiling.

"That was pretty," said Annie, never pausing as she served up the food she had cooked all morning.

"I don't even know what song I played!" whispered Laura.

"It was 'Wildwood Flower,'" said Annie. "It was one of your mother's favorites. Now, go ahead and sing it."

"I can't sing, Annie! Plus, I don't even know the words."

"Hush, girl. Just do it!"

Laura hushed. And much to her surprise—just did it.

GOT ANOTHER BISCUIT?

Kin and Laptop watched from the pit wall as the cars roared past, one by one.

The first few cars ran in the low 160s. But as the morning dragged on, the speeds dropped.

The announcer called out a "159.78" as a sleek red, white, and blue Chevy finished its qualifying run.

Cope and Junior joined the two boys on the wall.

"They're going slower and slower," Junior said.

"That's good, right?" said Kin. Waddy still had to qualify. He was almost last on the list.

"Not necessarily," said Cope. "It just means the track is getting slower."

"Slower?" asked Laptop. "The track doesn't go anywhere. How can the track be slower?"

"It's just an expression," said Junior.

It seems like everything's just an expression, thought Laptop. *Why don't grown-ups just say what they mean?*

"It means the track heats up and the tires don't stick as well," said Kin, proud of his new knowledge of racing. "Cars run a little faster on a cool track."

Cope pointed up toward the bright blue empty sky. "All we need's a few clouds, and we'd be copacetic."

Laptop slid down from the wall.

"Where you going?" Kin asked.

"It's a secret," Laptop said as he ran off into the infield.

"Worf!" said Scuffs, following.

The little pond was in the very center of the race track, hidden from the crowd by the weeds.

In here, you could almost imagine you were alone. Only the snarl and howl of the racing engines reminded Laptop that he was at a race track.

He stood by the muddy edge of the pond. He looked all around in the weeds. But no one was there.

He leaned over and looked down into the water.

Not even Moby Cat. The shadow of the giant catfish was nowhere to be seen.

"Dell!" he whispered. "Are you there?"

No answer.

"Darn!" said Laptop. He sat down in the mud. He felt like crying.

Then he heard a strange rustling noise, and a distant voice, almost like a whisper:

"Hey, kid. That dog have a name yet?"

Laptop jumped to his feet. He looked all around again for his friend, the Civil War soldier, Delbert, or Dell.

Then he saw the shadow.

"There you are!" said Laptop. "I need your help."

"Help . . ." repeated Dell, or rather, Dell's shadow. He sounded almost asleep.

"Remember that thing you did with the clouds this morning? Could you do that again?"

"The clouds . . ." Dell sounded weak.

"You know, make the clouds appear!" said Laptop.

"Maybe," said the soldier. "It's hard, though. Especially in the daylight."

- - - - - - - - - - - - - - -

"Will you try? It's important!"

"I guess. Got another biscuit? I need something to perk me up."

"I thought you couldn't eat. Being, you know, a ghost and all."

"Eat?!?" Dell sounded disgusted, or at least as disgusted as it was possible for a shadow to sound. "It's the smell that does it for me. The smell of good old-fashioned country cooking. It gives me the power I need. Otherwise, I get sort of vague, you know."

"Hmmmmm!" said Laptop.

"Worf!" said Scuffs.

Dell shrugged, or rather, his shadow shrugged. "So how about a biscuit? Hey, where you going?"

"I can do better than that!" said Laptop as he ran off through the weeds, with Scuffs right behind him.

"Dad's coming up soon," said Junior. "But we aren't going to beat those early times unless we get some shade."

He looked up. The sky was bright blue.

Kin shook his head. He wished he could help. There was more to racing than he had ever dreamed. Even the weather!

The next racer to qualify was Kyle Petty.

"He's the son of a legend and the grandson of a champion," said Junior. "His grandfather was one of the first professional stock car drivers, and his dad, Richard Petty, was the King."

Kin nodded. He remembered learning that the King was *not* Elvis, not here at the track anyway.

Kyle Petty's car streaked across the finish line.

The crowd in the grandstand cheered as the announcer gave his speed: "Kyle Petty, 160.56."

"That's a little slow for Kyle," said Junior.

"We could still get the pole with a little luck," said Cope.

"I'm up pretty soon," said Waddy. He looked at Junior and Kin. "Why don't you boys run over to Annie's and bring me a cup of her coffee?"

GHOSTS ARE NOT DEPENDABLE

"Amazing," said Junior. He and Kin were standing in the line at Infield Annie's.

Laura was sitting on the counter, singing "Stand by your Man."

"She's almost as good as the late, great Tammy Wynette! What a voice! Why didn't you tell me your little sister was a country and western singer?"

"I—uh—I didn't know myself," said Kin. "It's kind of a new thing."

Even though Laura had been playing most of the morning, she was still surprised that her fingers found the chords.

She was even more surprised that her voice

seemed to know all the words, and the tunes, to songs she had never even heard before.

And could hit all the notes!

But most surprising of all was how much she enjoyed entertaining people. Laura loved singing and playing to a crowd and making them smile. She loved hearing their applause and cheers.

It didn't matter that it was just a small crowd—the racing fans standing in line for Infield Annie's Southern cooking.

The line was getting longer as the day got hotter. There was her big brother, Kin, and his new friend, Junior.

Junior seemed to like the music. Kin looked as surprised as Laura was.

Laura was just finishing "I Got Over You Again Today" when she saw something small and fast streak into the booth, ducking under the counter.

There was another small, fast yellow streak right behind it.

Laura looked behind her. "Laptop?"

It was her little brother and the little yellow dog.

Annie was serving Laptop a plate of greens and beans and corn bread.

"I thought you wanted a hot dog," she said.

"Changed my mind," said Laptop. He sounded out of breath. "Throw on a biscuit," he said to Annie. "Thanks!"

He streaked off under the counter again.

"Hey!" Annie called out after him. "That dog have a name yet? A dog's got to have a name."

"Scuffs," Laptop yelled back.

"Worf!" agreed Scuffs as he followed Laptop into the crowd.

Laptop ran at top speed through the weeds, with Scuffs right behind him.

He skidded to a stop beside the little pond.

"Delbert? Dell?"

No answer.

Ghosts are not very dependable, thought Laptop.

He looked all around, squinting to block the sun from his eyes. It was no use. The shadow of the Civil War soldier was nowhere to be seen.

Laptop sat down on the ground beside the pond. He looked up. There wasn't a cloud in the sky.

Darn, he thought. Then he heard the loudspeakers crackle, and the boom of the announcer's voice:

"The next racer will be the Ford Taurus owned and driven by Waddy Peytona of Jeptha's Knob, Kentucky."

"Worf!" said Scuffs, jumping up.

"Okay, okay!" said Laptop. "You go on, Scuffs. But I'm waiting here."

"Worf!" said Scuffs as he hurried off through the tall grass.

"I just hope Dell comes through," muttered Laptop.

POLE POSITION

"Where'd you go?" Kin asked. "Where's Laptop?"

"Worf!" said Scuffs, who had run at breakneck speed from the pond in the weeds to the pits.

"Well, never mind," said Kin. "Just stay here with me out of the way."

The Waddy Peytona Racing Team was getting Waddy's Ford ready to run. A crewman pulled a wire from a plug on the rear bumper.

"What's that wire for?" Kin asked Junior.

"It's connected to a heater that keeps the oil warm," said Junior. "That way the engine doesn't have to warm up. Daddy's up to speed right away."

"What does warm oil have to do with speed?"

"Everything has to do with speed," Cope said to Kin. "The moving parts of an engine, the pistons and valves, are set to very close tolerances. Metal expands when it's hot, and every metal expands at a different rate."

"In a racing engine, you have aluminum, steel, cast iron, all mixed together," said Tach. "It's only running exactly right when it's warmed up. But for time trials we only get a couple of laps, so we have to be ready to go right away."

"Look!" said Junior.

Kin looked off to the south, where Junior was pointing.

A cloud was coming over the mountain.

It filled the sky and covered the sun.

"Copacetic!" said Cope.

"I can't believe our luck!" said Junior. "If that cloud holds out for a few minutes, it will cool the track for Dad's run. We could pick up that extra second we need for the pole position."

"Wish me luck, boys," said Waddy as he strapped on his helmet and climbed into the window of the race car.

Cope fastened a protective mesh screen over the window as Waddy buckled himself into his seat and checked his two-way radio.

Then Waddy hit the switch and the engine roared to life.

GGRRRRRRRRRRRRRRRR!!!

The tires squealed as Waddy Peytona pulled out onto the track just as the previous qualifier was pulling in.

The 700 hp Ford sang a song of power as it accelerated around the first turn.

"We need to impress this new sponsor," Junior said. "I know he's up in the stands somewhere."

"And the pole position is that important?" Kin asked.

"It gives an edge," said Junior. "Plus, there's a thousand-dollar extra pole position purse put up by a brake shoe manufacturer. If we could collect that money, it would help."

Kin crossed his fingers. He wanted his new friends to win! "I know we can do it!" he said under his breath.

"We?" Junior looked at Kin curiously.

Kin reddened. He hadn't wanted anyone to hear him. "I guess I sort of identify with the Peytona crew. If . . . that's okay."

"It's more than okay," said Cope, who had been listening in. "It's . . . "

"I know," said Kin. "It's copacetic."

Cope looked puzzled. "How'd you know what I was going to say?"

There was a sudden crackle on the two-way radio.

"There's Dad!" said Junior. He handed the radio to Cope.

"Are you reading me?" came the voice over the radio.

"Copacetic. How's she running, Waddy?"

"Loose but strong," came the answer. "Think this engine will hold up for one flat-out lap?"

"It will if you will," said Cope. "Put the hammer down and let her rip!"

Kin watched from the pit wall with Scuffs, fascinated, as Waddy accelerated into the first turn.

The blue and yellow Taurus seemed to stretch out like a greyhound as it ducked low into the corner and ran flat out down the long straightaway.

The unmuffled roar of the powerful Ford V-8 was like a song of power and speed.

Watching the sleek stock car, Kin felt a rush through his veins. He could almost imagine the thrill of powering it through the turns.

Someday I'll be out there driving! he vowed silently.

"Go, Dad!" Junior yelled into the radio.

"Copacetic!" said Cope.

"Go, Waddy," breathed Kin.

"Go!" whispered Laptop.

"Worf," said Scuffs.

Inside the car, Waddy Peytona concentrated on using his decades of carefully honed racing skills.

The Taurus drifted high toward the wall as it came out of the last turn and started down the straightaway.

Waddy Peytona listened intently to the song of his engine.

One misfire, and he would lose precious hundredths of a second. One valve bounce, and he would lose precious tenths of miles per hour.

So far, luck was with him.

Luck and the hours of work, years of experience, and vast quantities of talent Tach and Cope and the rest of the team had put into the car.

The finish line loomed ahead.

Waddy mashed the pedal all the way down. He felt the engine strain like a thoroughbred. He felt the tires grip on the cool track . . . pushing the Ford over the line.

"Hooray!" he yelled to himself over the roar of the engine and the roar of the crowd. The time wasn't yet official, but Waddy Peytona had been driving race cars for twenty years.

He had a feeling. And Waddy had learned long ago to trust his feelings.

KIDS' STUFF

"Hooray!" said Annie.

"Was it that good?" Laura asked as she finished her last song and put her guitar aside.

"You were fine, honey," said Annie. "But I wasn't cheering for you. I was cheering for my old friend Waddy Peytona. He just won the pole!"

Laura knew what the pole position was from her grandfather. But she had been so wrapped up in her singing that she had missed the announcement.

"I haven't been listening to the announcer," she said.

"Neither have I," said Annie. "But I can tell by the faces."

"Faces? What faces?"

"Look."

Annie pointed toward the pits. The entire Waddy Peytona Racing Team—plus Kin and Scuffs—was crossing the infield toward Infield Annie's.

They all wore wide grins. Even Scuffs.

"You fellows look happy!" said Annie.

"Better than that!" said Cope. "We just won the pole—163.64!"

"Congratulations," said Annie. "I'll bet you guys are starved!"

"We sure are," said Waddy.

"Who won second position?" asked Annie as she served up steaming plates of corn bread and beans. "Kyle? Jeff? Texas Terry?"

"Steve Gregson," said Junior. "I guess Hotshoe's hot new camshaft is working. Gregson's never been much of a contender before. 'Course, I wouldn't want him to hear me say that."

"'Course not," said a familiar voice.

They all turned and saw Hotshoe Hunter, who had just walked up.

"Gregson's Pontiac is the one to beat tomorrow," said Hotshoe. "You'll see."

"Bring him on," said Waddy with a laugh. "We'll be ready for him tomorrow. Say, Kin . . . "

"Yessir?"

- - - - - - - - - - - - - - - - -

"Did you boys ever come up with a name for that little yellow dog?"

"Worf!" said Scuffs.

"You missed the show," Kin said to Laura after the Waddy Peytona team had gone to take their car from the pits to the garage. "The time trials were great."

"She didn't miss the show, she *was* the show," said Annie. "This girl has a real talent for country music."

"Where's your little brother?" Hotshoe asked Kin.

Kin shrugged. "He and Scuffs ran off somewhere."

"Worf!" said Scuffs, looking off toward the infield and wagging his tail.

"Well, you kids better go find him," said Hotshoe. "I'm going to stay here and help Annie clean up."

"You kids stay away from that pond in the weeds!" Annie called out.

"Why?" asked Hotshoe as the kids ran off.

"I've heard stories," said Annie. "There's supposed to be a catfish big as a rowboat in that dirty old pond."

Hotshoe laughed. "Annie, that's just a tall tale. Sometimes I think you would believe anything!"

* * * * *

Kin and Laura followed Scuffs through the high weeds to the center of the infield.

They found Laptop sitting by the pond. Next to him was an empty paper plate.

"I thought you didn't like Southern cooking," said Laura.

Laptop shrugged. "I don't. I've been feeding the fish."

"There aren't any fish in this old pond!" said Kin. "It's too little."

"Oh yeah? Watch," said Laptop.

He sailed the dirty paper plate out over the water.

"You shouldn't be littering!" protested Laura.

The paper plate hit the water, and suddenly the surface of the pond erupted in a huge splash—and the plate was gone.

Kin jumped back.

"Worf!" said Scuffs.

"What was that!?" Laura asked. She had seen a gray shape, a row of teeth—and that was all.

"Moby Cat," said Laptop.

"Nonsense," said Kin. "Must have been a bunch of

minnows or something. Let's head back. Grandpa's waiting."

"You missed all the excitement," said Laura as she helped Laptop brush the mud off the back of his pants. "You missed the time trials, and my singing, too."

"I heard your singing," said Laptop. "Some of it, anyway. And I didn't care about watching the time trials. I just wanted Kin's friend's dad to win."

"He did, too," said Kin. "Thanks to some lucky weather."

"I know," said Laptop. "I've been hanging out here with my new friend, Dell."

Kin tapped his head and smiled. "Laptop's talking about his imaginary friend," he said to Laura as they started back toward Hotshoe's trailer. "The ghost of a Civil War soldier, no less."

"He's no more imaginary than you are!" said Laptop.

Laura took Laptop's hand. "There's nothing wrong with an imaginary friend," she said. "What did you two talk about?"

"Oh, you know, life and death. War and guns. Fate and destiny. Stuff like that."

"Typical kids' stuff," said Kin scornfully. "Come on, we have to get back to the trailer. Grandpa Hotshoe is waiting for us."

"Worf!"

The little dog was sniffing the mud by the pond.

"Come on, Scuffs!" said Kin impatiently. "Let's go!"

"Wait," said Laura. "He found something."

Scuffs began digging furiously. "Worf! Worf!"

He had found something shiny. He scratched it loose with his paws.

Laura picked it up and wiped off the mud.

It was a belt buckle, with crossed swords and three letters.

The second two letters were S and A.

The first letter was dented, as if it had been hit by a bullet long, long ago.

It could have been a U, or it could have been a C.

THAT ANGEL STUFF

That night the Travis kids went to bed early. Laura left her door open so they could talk. It was a habit they'd gotten into after their parents had died.

"So is the South as bad as you thought it would be?" Kin asked.

"I love it so far," said Laura. "I love being able to play and sing. But I still don't understand how it happened."

"I do," said Laptop from his top bunk. He put his SA belt buckle under his pillow with his computer. "My friend Dell explained it to me. He said that dead people have special ways of reaching out to the people they left behind."

"You mean, like Mom is teaching me?"

"Why not?" said Laptop.

"I don't believe that angel stuff," said Kin. "Particularly when it comes from a ghost!"

"Neither do I," said Laura. "But there is something strange going on. When I put my fingers on the guitar, I feel like someone is helping me play it. It's a wonderful feeling. Not spooky at all."

"You can have it," said Kin. "I'll stick with reality. Like a race car. Junior said I might get to help in the pits tomorrow."

"You kids quiet down!" called out Grandpa Hotshoe. "There's a big race tomorrow. I have to get up early and I need my sleep!"

"Good night," whispered Laura.

"Good night," whispered Kin.

"Good night," whispered Laptop.

"Worf!" whispered Scuffs from under the bunk bed.

More later . . .

About the Author

T. B. Calhoun is the pseudonym of an experienced mechanic who has written on automotive topics as well as penned award-winning science fiction and fantasy novels. Like Darrell Waltrip, Jeremy Mayfield, and other NASCAR stars, Calhoun is a native of Owensboro, Kentucky. He currently resides in New York City.